The Treasures of Her Heart

Camille Smith

Contents

Dedication

For my brothers, Robert, and Nathaniel.

Copyright

insert plain page

Chapter One

Her sun-kissed skin was warm from the fierce heat of the sun. A week ago, she was pale, uninspired, and slightly down in the dumps. Now she smiles, a contented grin spreading across her face, as she positions her face towards the bright healer in the sky. She wears a bright orange bikini, which compliments her golden skin. Finally, she can breathe deeply and release the chains of monotony. There is no sitting in the hotel room or being couped up anywhere. All four walls dissolve, opening to the big, blue sky, so vast and limitless. She lies there like a happy cat, content to bask in the sun. Memories of heavy winter coats and weeks of grey skies, pass through her mind, but she sighs them away, feeling the intense rays penetrate her skin.

The wind whips around her, and the palm trees sway wildly, yet she remains still, as though she herself has grown roots in this space. She is determined and adamant to embed herself and remain unperturbed and unmoved. Reclining on the sunchair, a cold pineapple juice in one hand, she feels as though this moment is endless and could stretch into infinity. The sheer comfort and ecstasy of this makes her feel like a queen in a classical painting. She reclines and eagerly etches herself on the canvas of life, in all fullness and beauty. As she closes her brown, slightly amber eyes and leans back, it sounds like when you hold a shell up to your ear. The rushing of the waves and the constant flow of wind make it all merge into one. The peaceful sky and wild sea stirred together in the wind; a restful restlessness juxtaposed in the physical world that seemed to seep into her spirit.

Momentarily, she glances at the other guests at the resort, most of them just like her. The sun seekers escaping dreary winter days. A couple of people appear interesting and attractive. She has to avert her eyes from a handsome, well-built man who appears to be tall and athletic. His skin is beautifully tanned. He has quite a prominent nose, and he seems to be maybe ten or so years older than her, yet she feels an intense attraction to him. It appears to make it worse when you attempt to avoid someone that you are attracted to. Your mind compensates with wild imaginings and passionate encounters, and it fixes more mystery on the object of your desire. The very presence of him makes her heart skip a beat. She notices other women making a beeline for him, more attractive women. She resigns herself to the fact that she has not got a hope in hell for these fantasies coming true. But she will enjoy them anyway. Uh-oh, their eyes meet as he departs the beach.

She became numb and breathless. It was like he had stolen her thoughts, and they were magnetised, stretched to wherever he went. She became transfixed, unable to form words, and barely able to conjure thoughts that were not about him. Now, she just desperately needed to see him even at a distance or be close to him. The powerfulness of his presence pervaded her being. Imagining the strength of his hands over her body. She had goosebumps just thinking about it. What does he smell like? Taste like? How passionately does he kiss?

The sound of his voice, would it send ripples of excitement down her spine? Where did he go? She wonders. That could be the last time she sees him, it could be his last day here. It feels like a tragedy to her, even though she doesn't know him and has not spoken to him once. She does not want to leave the beach. There is too much sadness in this moment. She knows that she must move now and shake it off. Try to shake him out of her mind. But part of her wants to go where he might be, go seek him out. Go and find 'the blood connection', that since breaking out of the womb we want to be connected in some way, in a raw way to hear another's heartbeat and the rush of blood pumping, flowing and echoing, like the ceaseless rush of the sea. The first moments of connection are akin to listening to a foreign language, it all seems unfamiliar yet fascinating. The lovers navigate secret yet primal pathways towards their goals. It is a silent navigation though, filled with momentary glances, leading to an intimacy unparalleled in other daily encounters.

There is also the underlying dread that the desirous intentions are unrequited. For instance, did she read the signs and signals properly? The rejection that she felt as a child, as her father departed from her life, never to return, still stinging in her mind. These triggers threaten to overthrow her rational mind and propel her into a sensitive and emotional state. This must be avoided, the relaxed holiday mindset maintained. The best strategy is to avoid said handsome man and in a resort of one thousand guests, this is possible.

Chapter Two

A walk is the best option to clear one's head. There were two routes to take a walk, the left shorter than the right. She was still full from her previous breakfast of scrambled eggs, French toast and salad. Happily, she embarks on a leisurely walk before the crowds assemble. Later in the day you must endure the mirage of flesh, wobbling beside the waves. Ahh, the peace and "reckless abandon" her favourite lyrics from the 'Temper Trap'. This is it, right? All those long working hours and that tedious daily commute were worth it.

The palm trees swayed in the gentle morning breeze. In the distance, far over the sea, dark clouds loom, like an ominous army waiting for the signal to fight. But she remained unperturbed, walking onwards. Half the sky looked as though it has been split in two, the bright blue versus the dark grey. She closes her eyes, as her feet sink into the sand. They should prescribe this as therapy. There was something so delectable about bare feet touching the softness of sand and the earth bearing your weight, taking the pressure of your body and all those unnecessary worries away. It was all about evaporation here; the heat, salty air, and waves giving a sense of renewal and refreshment. It was ever changing and yet all the same, an unnerving but reassuring paradox.

It is funny that we escape the greyness of the city: all those grey stone buildings, pavements, roads, and the dark, rain filled clouds above. Grey or beige - what dreary and dull colours. Her work outfits also reflected the city colours, wearing either black or grey. But now she was always in brighter colours, dresses that flitted around in the breeze gently, like the wings of a butterfly. The city was her cocoon, and this resort was the place where she broke free and spread her wings in a much-needed transformation.

Also, sunshine filled places seem to have buildings reflecting the vibrancy and energy, you see bright colours or gleaming white everywhere. It is so uplifting for your eyes and mind. She remembers seeing a video online stating that it is important to make your living space and surroundings, not only comfortable, but beautiful. It did not come to her naturally because she was constantly seeking that beauty in the castles back in the United Kingdom. Robert Adam was her favourite architect, especially his famous staircase at Culzean castle. They knew how to do interior design then; everything was ornate and measured. The complexity of design was in the wallpaper, cushions, fireplace, ornaments, and even the ceilings. Nothing was lifeless and dull. It was a feast for the eyes and the mind. That is what she wanted daily, a delicious feast for the eyes.

Talking about delicious, she looks up as she is approaching the resort on the way back and by the volleyball net, there he stands. The tall, tanned, and handsome man, which had stolen her heart earlier on. She feels her heart skip a beat, and it races, faster and faster. He notices her, especially as it is so quiet. She looks down, trying to avert her eyes, but it is hopeless. The pull strengthens like a star ship tractor beam, and she lifts her head. They are within touching distance now. He was in the middle of stretching but stopped abruptly. Does he feel the same way, or is he reacting to my weird body language? Do I look odd? She suddenly feels self-conscious, which adds to her nervousness.

Chapter Three

"Hi," she wants to wave, but stops herself, feeling that it would be too childish. He smiles, "hello." His accent is foreign, but she cannot place it. "Do you speak English?" It always feels terrible to ask this, as though the expectation for everyone to speak English comes off as awfully arrogant. "Yes," he replies. A one-word answer does not bode well. Here it is, then, the fantasy is always better than the reality. She had imagined a riveting opening conversation, and this was anything but. "Have a nice day," she states in a strained voice whilst waving happily like a pre-schooler, almost skipping across the sand towards the beach bar.

Just swallow me now, soft white and warm sand. Just swallow me. She skipped off so quickly that she only just heard him say, "you too." Great, now he must think I am a weirdo. Her mouth is parched, and she is happy to be at the bar, finding a nice secluded spot where she could watch the waves in the distance and not be too disturbed by other people.

A server approaches, and she attempts her best Spanish, "Un cafe, por favor. No leche. Gracias." The server smiles, appreciating her efforts. She still thinks that she is pronouncing "gracias" incorrectly. She looks around for a distraction, her phone locked away in the safe along with everything else. The freedom of not carrying absolutely anything was magical. No phone to be hooked onto, as though it were a drip keeping her alive. Of course, it is a shock but mostly it is a relief to be disconnected and unhooked. Right now, however it would be preferable to drown this discomfort with some pre-Raphaelite art and the poetry of Keats. Ahh! The fuel for the hopeless romantic. The tragedy of romance, in taking love too far.

The server brings her coffee, carefully setting down the cup and sugar container with a napkin. He gives her a quick smile as she thanks him. She remembers working in the Tennis and Health Cafe at Wentworth Golf Club as a waitress. One accident sticks out in her mind, she tripped and spilled the coffee on the table and the patrons just sat eyeing her in the evilest way, making the situation, almost unbearable. It is shocking how rude some people can be, there was no excuse for it either. Anyway, ever since then, she goes out of her way to treat everyone with respect regardless of job title, status, etc.

She takes the packet of brown sugar, gives it a little shake and tears the corner, then pours it into the steaming dark pool. Immediately, her body relaxes. There is something about a hot beverage, even before you drink it, that soothes the soul. Her mother would always prescribe tea whenever anxiety would take hold, or some drama would arise. Out comes the teapot, colourful tea cosy and biscuits. It seems a shame not to carry on the very British tradition.

She slowly sips the coffee, while listening to the lapping of the waves. Her mind wanders into a daydream. They say that it is important to let children daydream, not to disturb it, it has something to do with creativity and the mind resting. The sunlight pours through the leaves of the palm trees overhanging the sunbeds. It is busier now. People are chatting, reading, laughing and soaking everything in.

Nowhere else on this beautiful planet, I would rather be, she reflects. Little did she know, but the dark grey cloud, that was looming over the sea, is pretty much overhead now. Suddenly, the rain pours down in heavy sheets. Most of the people on the sunbeds are caught by surprise, hurriedly securing their belongings and heading for the shelter of the beach bar. Luckily, she can happily stay sat in the same position, courtesy of the overhead canopy, protecting her from the worst of it.

The bar fills up and people are chatting excitedly, as they wait for the downfall to pass. This isn't like Edinburgh where the rain can last for hours or all day, this is the Caribbean where it rains for about ten or twenty minutes at a time.

An older couple ask to sit at the table with her and she obliges politely. They ask her where she is from and how long she is staying, the usual questions. She has learned from previous encounters to keep people at a polite distance just in case you dislike them and must avoid them everywhere around the resort.

Boundaries are so important, children at school should be taught this, for multiple reasons; for instance, to enter and maintain respect in their friendships, relationships, family life and in the workplace. Emotional intelligence is just as important as academic intelligence. If you grow up without healthy examples of relationships or positive role models, then it is just an uphill struggle through life's various relationships, littered with multiple mistakes.

Chapter Four

The bar was getting too crowded for her liking, so she says her goodbyes to the cute, elderly Canadian couple and gets ready to face the deluge back to her room. The rain is unforgiving, soaking her dress completely. However, it is exhilarating though. She looks down at the puddles and does not notice the handsome stranger and bumps right into him. Her hands touch his rippling six pack, as she pulls back from him.

"Oh, I am so sorry. Uh... the rain." He nods and smiles, "it's okay." They stand for a moment just looking at each other, not knowing what to say. Another awkward exchange. She notices the rain dripping from his prominent nose and down his muscular arms and very toned body. Wow. The chemistry was undoubtedly there. Then she blurts out, "are you here alone?" He replies, "yes and you?" "Uh, yes." Just being near him was making her dizzy. A consequence of the pheromones. She remembers reading an article describing how a ridiculous percentage of attraction was down to pheromones. She stops herself from deliberately sniffing as she thinks this.

Her body was now shivering, and he notices this and says, "you should go and get dry, if I had a towel, I would..." He pauses and she smiles, both of their imaginations were going to the same place. Here is to synchronicity. "Thank you," she gives a coy, flirty smile. "Do you fancy a drink later? At the lobby," he says smoothly. "Sure, what time?" She replies, biting her lip to stop it from shaking. "Seven." "Okay, see you then," she casually sweeps a stray strand of wet hair from her face and tries to walk confidently away. She wants to see if he is watching her walk away, but the nervousness is overpowering. Therefore, she carefully walks as gracefully as possible, trying not to slip on the wet stone.

Chapter Five

The room was spacious with a high ceiling. What is it about lofty ceilings? They make rooms seem grand and amazing. It is like you have space for all your thoughts to just float away beyond reach. The balcony was brilliant. On her first morning here she stood outside listening to the unusual birds chirping and spotting the geckos racing across the bark of the tree. A giant flying insect with red wings flew towards her and broke up the serenity of that moment, as she had to rush inside while slamming the balcony door. Tropical holidays come with guaranteed bugs of course, although she read online that January has less bugs and humidity. She would have to skip the insect spray this evening though, it has such a strange odour, no matter how they try to fragrance it, it smells odd and doesn't mix with her favourite perfume.

There is something to having a signature scent. Her usual perfume is sensual, deeply fragrant and delicious. When she wears it, she feels like an empress of luxury. That is what perfume should do; transform you, elevate you, lift you up and make you feel incredible. The perfume transforms you into a sensual goddess, who smells divine. Along with the right outfit and make up, of course.

She undresses, pats herself with a towel and stands naked in the room. The cleaners have done a good job, the Queen sized bed neatly tucked and the towels arranged into two swans. It is the little touches, you know, that make you feel special.

She walks to the wardrobe and looks at herself in the mirror, feeling her stomach and examining her tan lines. Her hands move over her dresses, reflecting on what one says glamorous and classy, but also fun and sexy. The pink one shows off her wonderful curves, but she has to fiddle with the straps. There is nothing worse than a dress or outfit that you have to constantly adjust while wearing it, to feel comfortable. No. The red one, it is short and playful but doesn't emphasise her bosom. No. The white one, it goes in at the waist nicely with lovely lace detail, emphasises her breasts, is short enough and matches her gold heeled sandals so well. Plus, her gold jewellery finishes it off, just like that. Yes. This one. Yes! Mwah. She blows kisses to herself in the mirror and dances over to lie down on the bed.

The sheets feel so soft against her slightly sunburned skin, it is soothing. She sighs as she runs her fingers across her smooth skin. *Suddenly* Goosebumps rush over her and her nipples harden. Some people are more sensual than others, the slow, gradual touch preferred; building up to a climax, rather than the straight to it pneumatic drilling. She wanted sensual intimacy, the enjoyment of the race, not just reaching the finish line. She kissed a friend once, it was nice but there was no real chemistry on her side. It had to be there, the spark of passion that ignites the flame of true connection. Without it she imagined it would just be like going through the motions. Eww, nothing worse.

It would be better to binge watch a series, eating crisp sandwiches and cupcakes. Mmm, that is what she misses here, crisps. They have a new flavour for her favourite brand, prawn cocktail, and they are just mouth wateringly good. Oh, and on the crisp sandwich side, something possibly very British - it is important to try grated cheese and crisps in a sandwich together. There is something about the mix of textures that is sensational. Once you go there, you will never go back. A sandwich is not a good sandwich without crisps crushed inside it.

There was a time when she lived on peanut butter and cheese melted inside a baguette or bagel. It had to be grilled or toasted for the full effect. Her mouth was watering just thinking about it. She tried to be a vegan and was successful for six months, but is now a flexitarian, which is another term for being a lazy vegan.

Order room service or go to the buffet? This is the most important question right now. The day had taken its toll and another wave of rain was tapping gently on the roof. She curled up and dragged the firmer, decorative cushion under her head. Thoughts came and went; nothing was sticking and eventually sleep came upon her.

Chapter Six

When she awoke an hour later, she noticed that the sunlight was back, no ominous grey clouds. What time is it? She groggily moves across the bed and presses the digital display on the wall- '14:00' flashes bright blue. Her stomach grumbles, but her thoughts are on a nice, steaming cup of coffee, that she could enjoy peacefully on the balcony, before entering the busy buffet, filled with bronzed bodies.

The coffee maker and pods await. It is socially more acceptable to sit on the balcony with clothes on, right?! How nice it would be to feel comfortable enough to be naked all day long. She puts on a comfortable satin wrap, which clings to her body, sending ripples of pleasure to her core. There is something about delicate materials on the body, cascading materials which float in lightness. Light clothes alleviate the burden of wearing heavier material. To think that women used to be imprisoned in corsets and heavy fabrics, as though gravity were not enough to keep them in their place.

It is a relief now, that there is much more openness in relation to fashion. Freedom to be comfortable in your own skin. The external acceptance of who you are which makes the internal acceptance, easier. Many of us live in a state of self-denial, due to social conventions and norms. Shame is everywhere and that is a sad shame.

She shakes her head at these thoughts, while the coffee maker whirrs loudly, spitting out the hot black potion with a nice foam covering. The balcony chairs are a dark green plastic, practical but they look like cheap garden centre furniture. Regardless, she languishes her body on the hot seat like a lazy cat. She remembers in Peru, a stranger told her that sitting with your legs crossed (which is considered more lady like) was actually terrible for certain ligaments and the hips. Since then she has slightly splayed herself and to be honest, it is far more comfortable. Unfortunately, the backs of the plastic chairs are uncomfortable, this will be a short coffee break then.

The buffet closes at three pm to restock and refresh for dinner at six pm. She throws on a bra, vest top, knickers and shorts and pushes her feet into the sandals, that were purchased last minute at the airport. The warm air brushes against her face in a pleasing breeze. Her mind is still giddy from being asked out, but it is important that she stays grounded and does not get too swept away. The 'Tinder Swindler' on Netflix, those catfish documentaries and the increase of scammers in the world, would make anyone extra cautious while dating.

The world of online dating is now an absolute minefield; fake profiles, scammers phishing for information, accounts being replicated and hacked. Maybe speed dating is better because you can see them in reality, but even so always err on the side of caution. The statistics for sexual assaults and rape leading from online dating is shocking. She just hopes that schools have picked up on this and are teaching everyone how to stay safe online while asserting themselves. It is important to learn how to display clear emotional and physical boundaries. There always seems like more can be done in the world, to keep everyone safe.

Chapter Seven

"Hola," a friendly server greets her with a wide smile, breaking her chain of thoughts. "Hola," she replies, observing that the food hall is quite full. She quickens her pace, opting to grab her food before getting a table. Once her plate is loaded, she finds a nice quiet corner. Never one to eat like a rabbit, her plate is a mixture of pasta, salami, bread (with mustard) and some mashed potato. Buffets are the best for having the most surprising mixtures of food on one plate. Fifteen minutes later and she sits back happily sipping fresh pineapple juice. Waves of contentment flood over her, a nice full belly now, as she watches the cheeky little birds swooping in the hall, collecting leftovers.

Contentment is easy to hack- get enough food, sleep, sunshine, water, and exercise. Then attempt to be sociable, if you so desire. Do something for the body, mind and spirit, every day. Mix it up, be creative or get creative, to avoid the mundane. Of course, those annoying phases of anxiety and/or depression may surface. But just like you train your body, your mind needs some fine tuning too.

Positive affirmations are great, whether you believe them or not, saying "I am confident, I am beautiful, I am amazing and I am loved," multiple times a day. What harm can a little positivity do?

The resort service staff are shuffling around her now, clearing tables and setting them up for dinner service. She takes the hint and departs saying, "gracias, ciao."

The sunlight is bright on the white path, the walkway to the lobby teems with Iguanas, herons and turtles. Little groups are forming, with excited children staring at the turtles. She admires families that travel with young children and babies. People whispering in the airport queues, "let's hope we don't get the crying baby next to us." The lack of compassion towards children astounds her. It is no wonder that so many countries rank low for child and family satisfaction. First, teach tolerance, then elevate families to the precious status that they deserve. Without good solid family values, society does not have a good foundation to build upon.

The regular buggies are picking up people along the path, to take to the lobby. She waves the driver on. Not far now, the bright, white to enter ↑

wooden church beckons her. Inside it is nice and cool. The wooden image of Jesus on the cross, sits at the front. The comfy sofa like pews are soft. The denim shorts ride up a little and she pulls them down. The memory surfaces, "put your boobs away," her mother growls quietly during church service. She was a teenager just standing up straight in a comfy t-shirt, totally unaware that her body appeared offensive to her mother. Here comes the shame train again, pulling right into Complex station. The lifelong damage caused by the seemingly small comments, you really do have to watch what you say to children. Bowing her head, she prays.

Minutes pass and she finishes her prayers. The image of those cakes in the cafe fills up her mind. Mmm, a couple would be nice. This is the absolute joy of all-inclusive resorts, just flash your bangle and you can fill up your plate and cup. No messy cash or card transactions. On her plate is a beautiful pink macaroon, some cream filled puff pastry and a fruit filled tart, sitting ready to be consumed. The cakes and pastries glisten in delicious sweetness. She salivates, bringing the tart to her mouth taking a big bite. The sweet, stickiness on her tongue and lips is divine. Mmm, the sound unconsciously reverberates inside, like a reflex.

All food should be this good, never should anything taste bland. The senses should be tingling in delight, from the first look there needs to be an eager anticipation of pleasure that awaits you.

The clock on the wall chimes five times. Best walk back, grab a snack then get ready for the date. Although she opts to wear basic make up, painting her toenails and fingernails is a must to feel party ready. Plus the shower, preparing her hairstyle and shaving necessary parts. It is all time consuming and feels more like proper pampering, if done at a leisurely pace, rather than running about, like a headless chicken. Dates carry enough nerves with them, she wants to be ready and at the lobby bar by six fifty pm. Lateness is something to be ridiculed and despised. Punctuality shows respect to your company. All that rubbish about late people being more intelligent needs to be scrapped from existence. Lateness is a sign of absent mindedness and thoughtlessness. Rant over.

Chapter Eight

The walk back involved dodging more showers by sheltering under the trees. She shakes the sandals off her feet. It is such a relief to ditch the sandals again. Here is to, feet freedom. Her mind wanders back to the rippling muscles of Mr Handsome. Hold on, how shocking is it that she does not know his name.? He looks like a Daniel, no. James. Wait, the accent. Oh, there are too many unknowns here.

The dating preparations begin. An hour or so later and the look is complete. She admires herself in the mirror. Then she takes a couple of selfies and long shots, while her phone balances on the shelf. The red gloss glistens as she pouts. The alarm rings, six, forty pm. Time to depart.

Her gold, sandalled heels, clatter along the lantern filled pathway. Insects whirr and buzz everywhere. The cooler, evening air feels saturated with exciting possibility. At the lobby bar, she waits for her date. This place is like a wind tunnel. All up her arms goosebumps tingle, while the light fabric from her dress flutters around wildly. The clock above the neatly displayed rum and whiskey bottles reads, 'Two minutes past seven'. This is not a good start; he has thirteen minutes to show up and not a second longer. In her frustration she orders a Caribbean, tropical princess cocktail, it is a colourful concoction of rum and strawberry liqueur. A cute, pink umbrella sits on top. Cocktails should always be colourful, decorative, and fun, as a basic standard. One rock club in Reading that she frequented, served blue cocktails in pint glasses, which goes against everything that a cocktail should be. The bubble-gum taste was very moreish, however.

Sipping on the Caribbean, tropical princess cocktail, the alcohol starts swirling in her body. The weird giddy heaviness begins drowning the annoyance of possibly being stood up. A beautiful couple, settle down, a couple of seats away. A buggy pulls up to the lobby and she stands up tall overcoming the light-headedness. She stomps loudly with her sandals, slumping down onto the buggy's blue plastic sponge cushions. Next destination, beach bar.

Let us hope that he is not on the walkway. There are only two excuses that she would accept for lateness: an injury/near death experience or helping someone in need. It is important to command respect, not demand respect. The air whizzes by, adding to the dazed but extremely calm state of mind and body.

The beach bar has swings on the second floor, she hops off the buggy, heads up and sits on one of them. Swinging happily while tracing the constellations in the night's sky. Orion, again. The belt gleaming. A couple walk past, the woman with short, bobbed blonde hair gives her a lovely smile. It is amazing when people do that, spread their joy and goodness. She beams back at her. A nice form of solidarity. The world needs more of this, please.

She swings

Now, skipping to the bar, feeling like a teenager after being in the park, she orders a Cuba libre (rum and coca cola). Usually the strict rule of no caffeine after four pm applies, but it was a wild, no rule, kind of night, so anything goes. Surprisingly, the earlier jilting doesn't appear to bother her much. Rejection is a thing, if you make it a thing. Rationalise it and realise that it never is as personal as you believe and voila - it evaporates. Oh, rejection and fear of failure, how many dreams have you stolen from people's lives? Give a big, fat finger to those fears and you will be unstoppable.

She sits up on the stool, eavesdropping into the conversation which is happening next to her. The loud American accent slightly slurred from drinking, an Irish accent from a small, dark haired middle aged woman and a well spoken English accent reminding her of the Bond 007 films that she watched as a child.

Suddenly, someone taps her on the shoulder. "Oh," "Is this your hair clip?" "Yes. Thank you." The elderly man shakes as he passes it to her, the smell of whiskey hanging on the air as he speaks. "Have a good night." "Yeah, you too." The group next to her fall silent, witnessing this exchange. She looks up at them and smiles.

The American man, slightly heavy set, looks through blurred eyes, and holds his arms open. "Do I detect a slight Scottish accent, wee lassie?" He attempts his best Scottish but fails miserably. "Aye," she replies, "I was born and raised in England, been living in Scotland for ten years now." "There you go, Terry, a fellow country person for you." Terry raises his whiskey glass and attempts to say "cheers," but he is too intoxicated to speak. She nods and smiles, *now*

Chapter Nine

Suddenly, a woman bursts into the middle of the group, looking directly at her. "There you are, I have been looking everywhere for you," she exclaims this, while winking quite obviously at her. She is totally bemused by such behaviour, yet tipsy enough to go along with it. "Sorry, I got side-tracked. The swings, you see." "Well, you must make it up to me, our table is booked for eight thirty and we are already ten minutes late." "No, we cannot be late. Nice to meet you, I cannot be late." She stops herself from quoting the white rabbit from Alice in Wonderland: 'No time to say, hello, goodbye, I'm late, I'm late, I'm late'. Nobody needs to see the inner workings of her quirky brain.

The woman helps her from the bar stool and they rush away together down the stairs. They giggle together like excited schoolchildren. "Hi, I'm Cleo. I just had to save you." The Australian accent rings out. "Thanks. I think." She looks at Cleo, the long, red hair, flawless porcelain skin and blue green eyes. An imposing classical beauty, like the painting of Aphrodite or La Belle Dame Sans Merci. A stunning woman that would inspire Leonardo

Da Vinci or J.W Waterhouse. Her heart skips a little as she traces every outline. Plump, pink lips. The way her dress sits delicately on her curves. Everything about her was soft, amenable, and graceful. Effortless beauty. Cleo laughs showing a slightly gapped toothed smile. Her laugh is song like in quality. Am I dreaming? Or drunk?

Cleo exclaims, "let's go, my throat is as dry as the outback here. Our Mexican cuisine awaits." "Ooh, Mexican. I love Mexican." Her belly rumbles. Cleo takes her hand in such a familiar fashion. It is as though they had known each other for years. There was nothing awkward or uneasy in their connection. She felt strangely comfortable, calm and at ease. It appeared that Cleo's confident demeanour was soaking up, all doubt and nervousness.

They arrive at the Mexican restaurant. Cleo is trying to haggle with the server to squeeze us into the dinner service. She watches from a distance observing Cleo's skills: first the relaxed body language, as she leans on the counter. Second, the way that she positions herself beneath the server, looking into her eyes in a playful way. Third, the flashing of the smile. Finally, the well-spoken Spanish, then the passing of some pesos to sweeten the deal. Voila, a table for two. "Follow me, please." Cleo gives a cheeky wink in her direction.

They settle down and scan the QR code on the table to view the menu. Cleo orders a beer, and she orders a white wine, while fiddling with her gold painted nails anxiously. Cleo looks up from scanning the menu on her phone, "ahh, no phone. One sec, about done looking. I am having: Nachos to start then the Santa Fe chicken, finished off with ice cream." "Sounds good." Cleo passes her the phone. Their fingertips touch in the exchange. It is funny how certain parts of the body are more sensitive than others. The menu is simple, not too much choice. "The mini quesadillas look yummy, then the beef burrito followed by Crepes." "More decisive than I expected. At least you are not one of those people that, so devoid of imagination and identity, just copies the person that orders first."

The server takes their order then departs. Cleo states in her soft, Australian accent. "Where are you from?" "Ascot before now Edinburgh." "No way, I work in Surrey." "Seriously." "Wow, it really is a small world. Hey. Most people assume Australia, I only spent the first three years of my life there. What school?" "We moved around so much." "That really sucks." "Yeah, so many lost friendships. Pretty sure..." Cleo interrupts, "ahh, our drinks, finally." The server places them carefully on the table.

Cleo flashes that smile again, as she lifts her glass, "here is to new friendships. Cheers." "Cheers." They say that it is important to make eye contact while saying "cheers" for good luck. She looks straight into Cleo's blue green eyes, so clear and velvety, shining like a beautiful cenote. Infatuation begins to claw its way under her skin. Cleo takes a big gulp. Why is everything so fascinating about her? Each movement, word, and expression. Is this escapism through someone else? That itching desire to leave one's own body and thoughts, because living in your own brain becomes so tedious and tiresome. Time drifts more readily in such company. Or time vanishes altogether. The clock watching routine of what to do next in loneliness's void, dissipates. Pink luscious lips whispering, come closer, lean in, touch the wondrous and let the beauty melt and fuse into your skin.

She sips the wine in bigger gulps than usual to attempt to counteract her racing thoughts. Numb, numb; our desire to numb the discomfort. Are our emotions so difficult to withstand? She remembers learning about aversion therapy in GCSE psychology, whereby in order to get over a fear or phobia, you just face it head on. The premise is to awaken the patient to reality. To awaken the realisation that their fear was nothing. A phobia of dogs which came from being jumped on by a huge dog in the forest, she overcame by walking around deliberately in those parks, dominated by dog walkers. Self-imposed, aversion therapy.

Meanwhile, the fear of rejection filled her as a teenager, she would avoid eye contact and became anxious in crowded places. Well you know what to do, right? She deliberately took Drama classes to counteract her lack of confidence, this really did help. Performing on stage, large chattering crowds, all the adrenaline rush and excitement. If she gave into the fear, she would miss out those wonderful experiences.

"Hello, where did you go?" Cleo is waving her hand frantically. "Sorry, my mind has a tendency to wander." "No worries, our starter is coming." Cleo rubs her hands together happily. The white dress with big, red flowers is slightly low cut and a small scar is visible above Cleo's left breast. She tries not to stare at it but is curious, nonetheless. They both thank the server, exchange a "Bon Appetit" and begin tucking into their food. The white wine settles and that nice, floating feeling, descends. The meat in the quesadilla is mouth-watering and she closes her eyes, savouring the juicy consistency and flavour. Cleo sits, elbows on the table, scraping knife and fork over the plate while chewing loudly.

Table etiquette was important to her growing up. Manners were everything. Imagine an aristocratic lady in a grand estate, that or very close, minus the stables and vast inheritance. "You are so dainty, the way you eat. Very neat and quiet like a tiny bird." Telepathy alert! "I will take that as a compliment." "Don't let my looks deceive you, there is a vulgar punk rocker lying in wait. Ready to be a bad influence, princess." "Humph. Hahaha," she laughs midway through a sip, almost snorting the white wine over the table. "See, already. Not very dainty anymore, are we?" They laugh together, wildly.

Laughter. It is great, right? Especially, the laugh until you cry kind. Holding back the tears and pig like snorting. That friend at school or college that you had with the outrageous laugh, everyone trying to provoke that sound, then the whole class would be in stitches. The release from societal pressures; work, relationships, family life and political correctness. Laughter is the best stress relief. It is surprising that there are not more comedians and comedy films around.

They continue to giggle loudly, attracting a couple of smiles and multiple frowns. Cleo waves over to the couple casting annoyed glances at them, "do you want to join us? You both look like you could do with a laugh." They look away angrily in embarrassment. "That shows them, the poor repressed souls. How close are you to becoming that?" Her red painted fingernails beckon over in their direction. "Hmm," she grunts in reply, taken aback by Cleo's harsh callousness. Was it the alcohol causing her to act that way?

This scenario reminded her of when she used to be slightly obsessed with a work colleague. Her name was Rachel, and she had the aloofness of a cat. Prowling about, always looking beautiful, graceful, and untouchable. She would follow her about and give her back massages during lunch break. They were always talking about their secrets and gossiping about other work colleagues. Yet, upon attending another colleagues wedding party, Rachel displayed a darker side (one fuelled by alcohol). A dark, cruel, and mean Rachel. How easy it is to mistake the brooding types as having emotional depth, when actually they are the opposite: emotionally devoid and sick. Thereafter, the friendship dwindled, and she took to having her lunch break alone.

Now, glancing out the window, up towards the bright, full moon, sadness flows over her. It was the disappointment, as the fantasy plops open like a water balloon hitting concrete. The atmosphere had changed. How easy it is for that to happen? It should be a social rule, alcohol should be avoided at all costs, when first meeting others. It is preferable to be in a sober state, to communicate authentically. Otherwise, it is like trying to decipher emotions conveyed through text messaging. Now that is a completely different minefield. Bam, wrong emoji and you are down. The quagmire of modern relationships. We are all baffled by it, right? Estranged parents, a phone call away. College friends, a DM message away. IRL (in real life)- face to face connection lost. The phone is the conduit for connection now. The reliance on digital media, our crutch. Prescriptions and subscriptions fill our lives, it is all pill popping, binge watching and eating. Learned helplessness and dependency.

She once tried to find friends on a dating app. Never again. There is a level of perfection that she demands from other people that she never displays herself. The ego bursts forth, it is pretty much her way or the highway. No wonder then, that she struggles to make friends. Meanwhile, she criticises those people that come to dating with extremely elevated expectations. But they brandish their lists on social media. My date must have abs, bulging muscles, corporate career, own house, car, teeth, hair, must love my dog, kids etc. Good luck ticking all those boxes.

Anyway, the world is now flooded with the self-love, awareness and actualisation. Millions of influencers are making money from people's elevated levels of insecurity and low levels of self-esteem. Well, the beauty and fashion industry has been doing it for the last century. Why not cash in? She thought about being an influencer. Hahaha.

The silence between Cleo and her was intense now. At least lost in her thoughts and edible escapism, through the delicious Crepes, solace arrived. Shocker, that chocolate will do that. Cleo finally breaks the tension. "Do you fancy a game of pool? The teenage club is open until eleven." Cleo gives her a sweet look, her eyes wide, like one of those cute anime kittens. She makes her sweat a little, by pausing, but before Cleo's face could drop, she replies, "sure, sounds fun." Spontaneity is so much better because there is no time to form expectations or start overthinking everything to death. Just grab an idea and go with it. No hesitation, no doubt- just forward motion. Overthinking is also the killer of many dreams.

Chapter Ten

The teenage club is a cute painted room just next to the tennis courts. The bright yellow surfboard and neon lights, shine inside. The comfortable bean bags and soft mini sofas are inviting. In the far, right corner, there sits that football game, the one where you spin the players around to hit the ball. Two large pool tables, very well worn with cue sticks, the ends rubbed down to next to nothing.

"Mine is sticky," Cleo announces in annoyance as she examines the cue stick. "Ha, you drew the short straw on that one." "Ah, this is your revenge for making you feel uncomfortable with my comments at dinner, right?" They both look at each other and laugh. Thank goodness the tension has broken. She had been formulating a reason to get away, ranging from a stomach bug to expecting an important work call (the time difference helps in this case). However, the instinct to flee dissipates further, as the friendly competition commences. She is better than Cleo, due to previous work colleagues influencing her to play after her work regularly.

Luckily, no-one else enters and they get ~~the this private~~ place to themselves. They are both slightly giddy from the alcohol and Cleo switches into a very flirty mood, frequently brushing against her and making excuses to touch. The defences go down, the atmosphere shifts. She begins to flirt back. Another sly brush of the hand on her lower back sends shivers all over, she swings around catching Cleo in the act. Suddenly, the door whacks open, breaking up the intensity of the moment. A group of five teenagers, tall and loud, noisily enter the room. Cleo grabs her hand and whisks her out before any comments could be shouted in their direction. One teenager does a loud wolf whistle, stirred on by their reaction.

Her heart is racing so quickly. They both clatter in their heels down the path. "Your place or mine?" Cleo states confidently as if she has rehearsed that question." "Oh, uh. Yeah, you mean room? Right. Dunno. What do you think?" "Hmm. Nice to know I still have that effect." Cleo flashes a cute smile. She looks away coyly. "You can't act all shy now. The cat is out of the bag, lassie." There was something quite immature about Cleo's behaviour now, she couldn't quite put her finger on it, but something didn't seem right. "I think we both need some water and maybe just juice." "Yes, mum. I mean ma'am." Cleo extends her hand energetically and they go back to the beach bar swinging their arms, as though they had been best friends since nursery school.

They sit at the beach bar, and she manages to stop Cleo from ordering another cocktail, instead they grab a mocktail. It is best not to get too drunk in a foreign country with a complete stranger. She remembers on a tour of Cambodia after visiting the famous Pub Street, one of the tour group members delayed the whole group searching for his passport, believing that the woman that he had picked up in the club the previous night had absconded with it. Luckily, he had found it in the rubbish bin in his hotel room.

Cleo begins poking her in a really childlike way. The weird shifting behaviour is confusing her now. She was about to make an excuse to leave when a shrill like voice pierced through the air, almost screaming out, "Cleo May Anderson, you come here right now." Cleo's face dropped and her body tensed and froze like an icicle. The short lady with dark bobbed hair wearing light blue pyjamas stomped over angrily. The slight plumpness of her face became more visible under the electric lighting of the bar. The night moisturiser not fully rubbed in was glistening. The wrinkles and frown lines all prominent and her grey hairs were shining.

"You promised this would not happen again, Cleo." Her voice softens as she glances around, aware that more people are watching. "Come back to your room young lady." What? Young lady. A wave of discomfort and fear overcomes her now. No, no, no. How old was Cleo? She looked about mid-twenties judging by the dress, confident demeanour and make up. Oh no. The stories flood her mind, men going to jail or being called perverts. No way. She hangs her head now, all flushed. Cleo's mum addresses her now quietly, "I don't know what she told you, or if she did reveal her age, but Cleo is only fifteen." Those words form an anchor in her heart. She cannot speak. "I can see you didn't know. You are not the first. It is okay. Let's hope that she doesn't cause a scene like last time. Best that you just walk away now." She can only nod and shakily moves off the bar stool, clattering heavily towards the stairs. Cleo's sobbing was still audible but dies away as she descended the steps.

What a fool? What a stupid fool? How could I be so stupid? There is no point beating myself up now. This would all be avoided if Mr Handsome, now named Mr Tardy No-show, would have been punctual for the date. Shifting the blame is much better for now, until the shock has been absorbed.

Luckily, she has chocolate in her room. This situation calls for chocolate, a cup of tea and a (semi badly) dubbed Spanish film.

Chapter Eleven

The next morning, a particularly loud bird perched on her balcony, jolts her from her sleep. It is singing its little heart out, as if it were a contestant on one of those talent competition shows. Just like that slightly grumpy judge, she races up towards the window and roars. No next round for you, bird. A resort worker clearing up leaves and debris looks up in shock. Quickly she smiles, turning from what looks like a 'Dawn of the Dead' zombie into a normal resort guest. He smiles back and carries on sweeping.

What time is it? She wonders. It feels early. All night, she was tossing and turning. Thus, the desire to return to bed is overwhelming. It is a relief however, that no hangover was piercing daggers into her brain. The grogginess even masks the events of the previous evening, until the memories slowly surface. Why does she feel so guilty, it is not like she did wrong? Distractions are required now, to dispel these feelings. A full day of distractions. Maybe a day away from this beautiful five star resort. Whoever coined that phrase, "hell is other people" was totally right. The drama only began when she started seeking

anything

others, outside of herself or inadvertently falling into the path of others. Either way, a day of separation and independence is called for. It is no wonder that the Buddha gained enlightenment while in solitude. Time to become untouchable and self-contained. The empire of the introverts shall rise. Extroverted behaviour: consisting of unnecessarily loud and attention seeking behaviour, is overrated. The inevitable chaos that ensues from large groups of drunken egotists being together, equals lifetimes of regret. No thanks. The quiet, thoughtful, reflective life is preferable. Possibly, doing something worthwhile and noble. Surely having a tangible set of goals to grasp onto, is better than the empty hedonistic vapour, that modern society seems to encourage and support.

Back at her home in Edinburgh, she is the director of a creative content website. Her mother still looks down on it, of course. Nothing would ever be good enough, except being a lawyer. But there is no pleasing some people and you really have to let go of all that and fully start living for yourself. Stop caring about what other people will think. At the end of the day, you are the one living your life day in and day out, don't waste it by doing something you hate, just to impress others with a job title.

Ugh! '8:33' flashes on the blue digital clock display. Not bad. Breakfast will not be too crowded then. She rushes to splash her face with water, clearing some smudged mascara from under her eyes with wipes. The red dress that she wears, comes to her knees and is not tight, it hangs nicely. On go the sandals and away out of the door she skips, happy to feel the warm morning sunshine on her face. In Scotland, if it is not pouring with rain, then it is a good day.

Chapter Twelve

The buffet is quiet, ahh. Bliss. She fills her plate with scrambled eggs, French toast, and pancakes, pouring over some syrup and honey. Energy, that is what she seeks, sugary syrupy processed energy. She remembers an article which she read recently where university students are no longer hooked on alcohol, but rather sugar. Sugary drinks, sweets, and chocolate. It is an improvement over alcohol. The full plate is emptied quickly, while intermittently sipping through two cups of black coffee. Yeah, caffeine and sugar. What could we do without it?

Heading back to her room to change, she puts on another coffee. Caffeine again, we really are, artificially awake automatons. A world without caffeine, would be disastrous. If the doomsday clock ticks any closer, she has decided to stockpile coffee in her garden shed. It makes sense, if they ration coffee then the demand on the illegal market would be so high. She would just be another capitalist benefiting from war and chaos. No harm in that right. We never learn from the stupidity of our ancestors. If we did there would be no war or poverty.

Humanity is self-destructive, as though it were afraid to truly prosper. Just imagine the real progress we could make if we really tried. The self-sabotaging instinct that we have as individuals, comes out in the collective. Despondency and apathy equal atrophy of the human condition. The decay and rot must be cut off, like a gangrenous limb. In that moment, she notices the small Bible, peeking through the slightly open bedside drawer.

Staring at the Bible, she remembers being at the top of Ben Nevis, the highest mountain in Britain. There she had discovered a Bible in a plastic tub, kept inside a small cupboard in the rock. She imagined that it was for the people who became stranded and stuck. It was apt considering that Jesus Christ, came to save all those who are lost, stranded, and stuck, in their own sin. She wasn't sure if you could have a favourite disciple to read, but for her it was the gospel of St. Matthew. It comes as no surprise considering the mighty power of God, that the wisdom and truth contained within the word, far surpasses anything written by anyone else.

Nowadays, the world seems so full of lovers of themselves, seeking anything but God. The Bible alerts us to this. They rely on their own philosophy, considering themselves to be masters of their own lives, instead of surrendering their lives to God. She could not say much though. The world had swept her up and the lusts had drawn her away from the path. The chaos in her life that she experienced could be put down to every time that she sinned. It was time to fully commit to God, especially considering the drama of the previous evening.

Sitting on the edge of the bed, she holds her hands together and bows her head and begins to pray. Her voice quietly whispers, "Heavenly father, I come to you in the name of the Lord Jesus Christ. Please forgive me for my sins." Waves of emotion overcome her, as she sits quietly, communicating with God. "I know that I don't deserve forgiveness, but please forgive me." She lies in tears, as she becomes overwhelmed with emotion. She thinks about the vastness of God's love, that his only son Jesus, was sacrificed to save us from our sins. If we repent, our sins are forgiven and forgotten. The shame can be washed away, meaning that we don't have to walk about under the shadow of shame and guilt. These are weapons of the enemy to bring us down, so that we wallow and are consumed by darkness, sadness and depression. In this state, we cannot do God's will because we are paralysed by fear. Thus, repentance, prayer and reading the Bible, are vital. These are ways to be released from the grasp of the enemy and to enable the light to fill us, instead of the darkness.

She remembers about the gospel that says about putting on the full armour of God. Then after a quick search on her phone, she finds the passage and opens the Bible to read it. A deeper peace overcomes her, a peace that only faith can provide. Gratitude fills her heart and she reflects on the commandments described in the new testament- love God first with all your mind, heart and soul. Then everyone else. Be the light so that you can glorify God just by being. Other people will see your transformation and be inspired by it.

A smile rests upon her face as she reflects on how amazing it feels to be released from the endless seeking in the world. The outside distractions are empty and unfulfilling. In the age of noise and vice, a good spiritual detox is needed. To be a fully committed Christian in this day and age, requires ceaseless prayer and awareness, so that you serve only God and not the desires and will of the world. I mean all you need to do is look up the testimonies of people near the brink of death or going into complete self-destruction, then they discover Jesus and bam, they are saved and transformed.

Chapter Thirteen

The best example of a spiritual transformation was experienced by her friend, Freya, who was suicidal about a year ago. It came out later that Freya was carrying the depression for years. She carried some guilt for not seeing the signs of depression in Freya before the breaking point. Freya explained later that she disguised it well in smiles and people pleasing. This situation changed the way she treats people, as well as her attitude towards mental illness. Now she feels a deep compassion towards anyone struggling.

The situation started with Freya cutting off everyone that she knew; family, friends, work colleagues, even neighbours, until she was completely isolated. At first, there were the excuses, then ignoring calls and finally her number became blocked by Freya. She felt angry at being ignored but realised later that Freya was in so much pain, anguish and torment. In fact, Freya was trying to protect her friends and family because she didn't want to be a burden. But people who love you won't ever see you as a burden, you are allowed to share your problems and get the support and help, that you need and deserve. Shortly after, Freya's depression escalated, and the suicidal thoughts were becoming more prominent. The feelings of complete hopelessness, despondency and despair were overwhelming her. She was barely able to function, Freya described it as a heavy weight bearing down on her chest, especially apparent every time that she tried to motivate herself to do something. It was like being pushed back by some terrible, dark force.

Eventually, Freya allowed her to visit. Buzzed into her flat, she walks in, shocked that the Freya that she once knew, confident, energetic and smiling, was gone. Now Freya was shrunken, she hardly made eye contact and her voice was quiet and mumbling. Her brown curly hair was greasy, and her face was pale and puffy. She was wearing a dirty fleece and joggers. Dirty plates, clothes, and clutter was everywhere. She wanted to say so much to Freya, but she was just dumbfounded. They sat in awkward silence; she was waiting for Freya to spill her heart out. Thirty minutes pass, nothing. Finally, Freya mumbles, "I am tired," and ushers her out of the door.

This encounter plays over and over in her head, day after day. A few weeks pass and Freya actually answers her phone, and her voice sounds different now, still quiet but with more energy. Freya describes something about renewed spirituality. Instantly, she worries that it is one of those crazy online shams, the ones full of- this will transform your life and you can manifest all that you want. A feeling of anxiety sweeps over her as she ascends the stairs towards Freya's flat. The previous encounter still weighs heavily on her mind.

Freya stands at the doorway, smiling, her brown curls styled beautifully. She is wearing her favourite, 'Save the Bees' t-shirt. Entering the flat, she could smell her signature perfume, it reminded her of a Summer field filled with wildflowers. A sigh of relief almost audibly falls from her lips. Freya smiles at her as they enter the living room. She opens her arms and hugs her tightly. They both smile widely at each other and start laughing. The kind of laughing that is spontaneous and you do not know exactly why you are laughing. It is awesome when that happens, even when you connect with someone and smile widely. It is like a deeper spiritual connection, like my spirit is saying "I really like your spirit." It is great.

Freya gestures *for* her to sit *down* while she goes to the kitchen to brew a cup of tea. She notices a Bible, prayer book and notebook sat on the coffee table. She knew that Freya had grown up in the church, but it seemed that her faith took a back seat to her fast paced life. Career, dating, money and partying. But in that very vulnerable time something switched within her. Maybe it was prayer (something that many of us do when we are in turmoil). Or maybe she knew like most believers, that he is always there for us.

Freya waltzes back in with a big tray. "Can you get that please?" She states looking down at the Bible and notes. "Oh yes," she scoops them up and carefully places them on the table where the yellow lamp sits. "Thank you." Freya sits and sighs and they smile at each other measuring each other's energy. "You must be wondering..." Freya begins. "Yes," she replies. "Well, I have struggled most of my life with anxiety and depression." "Sorry I..." "Don't worry. I have been saved. He was calling to me all along, but I was so hung up on my own will and desire. He strengthens me and I am renewed and reborn through him." As she speaks these words, the joy on her face was evident. This is the power of Jesus Christ, right there, speaking out in testimony and now sipping on a sugary cup of tea.

Chapter Fourteen

You would think that the transformation of her best friend, Freya would propel her towards the same path. Unfortunately, the role as creative content website director, kept her the doing the will of the world. Freya eventually left Edinburgh and trained to become a Christian counsellor down in London. They catch up so rarely now but she sees all the new friends that she is making on social media. What matters most of all is that she is content and healthy? She is still staring down at the Bible in front of her as she reminisces.

Suddenly, she becomes aware of the pins and needles in her left foot, which is being squashed by her right leg. Sometimes it is funny the uncomfortable positions that we stay in. Much to the dismay of our bodies. As she massages the pins and needles out of her foot with one hand, the other hand is flicking through the Bible. It falls open at page 1079. Philippians, chapter 4, verse 8 jumps out at her, which states-

"Finally, brethren, whatsoever things are true, whatsoever things *are* honest, whatsoever things *are* just, whatsoever things *are* pure, whatsoever things *are* lovely, whatsoever things *are* of good report; if *there be* any virtue, and if *there be* any praise, think on these things."

This passage she read over and over. It struck her as so positive and motivating. There is that part in the Bible that says that the word is [→ of God] sharper than a two-edged sword. Hebrews, chapter 4, verse 12 pops up on her phone as she inputs those words, it states-

"For the word of God *is* quick, and powerful, and sharper than any twoedged sword, piercing even to the dividing asunder of soul and spirit, and of the joints and marrow, and *is* a discerner of the thoughts and intents of the heart."

Just by reading the word, her heart was being moved towards the truth. The world is [→ Modern, for example] promoting sin as good, [it is] everywhere that you look. Stealing is revealed as glamorous in heist films. Fornication, adultery and sensuality [is] promoted in many Hollywood movies. Violence is all over the news. She remembers a verse that the pastor at her church growing up loved to repeat every Sunday at service.

(handwritten: Move up ↗)

Isaiah chapter 5, verse 20-

"Woe unto them that call evil good, and good evil; that put darkness for light, and light for darkness..."

(handwritten: While thinking this she opens up her notes)

There is some comfort to be found in the rapid renewal and growth of the Christian community around the world. She opened up her notes and looked at a poem that Freya had sent her, years ago, called- Never Alone.

Dark paths, I traversed.
Leading me to the worst,
Times in my life.
Broken and bruised.
Terribly misused.
A mistake to believe,
I was alone in this strife.
You held my hand when I was bleeding.
Lying and crying on the floor.
You held my heart when
I was lost.
And I couldn't take it anymore.
You loved me,
In the deepest darkness.
And I followed you,
Into the light.
Thank you, Lord,
For your strength.
You put my heart right.

If you or someone that you know is struggling with mental health issues, depression and/or suicidal thoughts, there is help-

For free, confidential support 24/7:

Samaritans: 116 123

National Suicide Prevention Helpline: 0800 689 5652

These are the numbers for the UK, other countries will have their own numbers, a quick online search will enable you to locate them.

Please do not hesitate in seeking support, your life matters and please remember that God loves you and there are people that love you. Peace and love to you, always.

Printed in Great Britain
by Amazon

20172936R00036